For Mohamed, who lives for music. —PY

For my lovely son, Boren.
And many thanks to Harvey Chan, Cheng Wang and Jackie,
who gave me a lot of support in doing this book. —JPW

Text copyright © 2004 by Paul Yee
Illustrations copyright © 2004 by Jan Peng Wang

Groundwood Books / Douglas & McIntyre
720 Bathurst Street, Suite 500, Toronto, Ontario M5S 2R4

Distributed in the USA by Publishers Group West
1700 Fourth Street, Berkeley, CA 94710

We acknowledge for their financial support of our publishing program the Canada Council for the Arts, the Government of Canada through the Book Publishing Industry Development Program (BPIDP), the Ontario Arts Council and the Government of Ontario through the Ontario Media Development Corporation's Ontario Book Initiative.

ONTARIO ARTS COUNCIL
CONSEIL DES ARTS DE L'ONTARIO

National Library of Canada Cataloging in Publication
Yee, Paul
A song for Ba /by Paul Yee; illustrated by Jan Peng Wang.
ISBN 0-88899-492-3
I. Wang, Jan Peng. II. Title.
PS8597.E3S65 2004   jC813'.54   C2003-904879-9

Design by Michael Solomon
Printed and bound in China

A SONG FOR BA

...

PAUL YEE

PICTURES BY

JAN PENG WANG

A GROUNDWOOD BOOK
DOUGLAS & McINTYRE
TORONTO VANCOUVER BERKELEY

MANY years ago, Wei Lim was born in the Chinatown of a large city by the Pacific Ocean. The boy's mother died when he was an infant, so he lived with his father and grandfather.

Wei did not see his father much because Ba was a singer in a Chinese opera troupe. Back in China, Grandfather had also been a singer, and Wei hoped that one day he would be a star, too, just like his father and grandfather.

But Ba refused to teach Wei the traditional melodies, nor would he demonstrate the flowing body movements needed for the stage.

"There is no future for opera here in the New World," he declared. "The old men are heading back to China, and the younger generations spend their money at picture shows instead. You'll be better off getting a good education."

So it was in secret that Grandfather
taught Wei how to sing.

Everyone in Chinatown knew Wei's father. The old-timers came from all around to see him perform, because the familiar sounds and scenes of the opera transported them to their far-off homeland.

Ba always played the part of a great general. He wore thick-soled boots, a brace of four flags and a helmet. On stage, he would spin like a top to deflect waves of spears hurled at him. When warriors suddenly attacked from two sides, he would arch backward and flip over and then resume fighting.

Wei loved to go to the opera. When the curtain lifted, drums and cymbals crashed. An emperor and imperial princess shook out their generous sleeves and lit the stage with dazzling colors. White-painted faces showed scarlet red around the eyes, robes glittered with metallic embroidery and sequins, and headdresses gleamed from bands of pearls and beads and millions of tiny mirrors.

Wei listened to the tuneful melodies gliding off the Chinese cellos and the sharp beats clicking from the woodblocks. He heard the high voice of the princess dancing around the lower voice of the emperor. He knew that women did not perform in the Chinese opera, so men played both the men's and women's roles. His grandfather had always played the female parts, and he had taught Wei many of his songs. Wei had a high, clear voice, but he thought he would rather play the general. In his mind, he saw himself doing acrobatic jumps, spins and twists just like his father.

One day, Grandfather announced, "I'm returning to China. I'm old now, and I want to see my hometown one last time."

Wei felt as if he were losing his best friend. "Please don't go," he cried.

Grandfather shook his head. "You shouldn't worry," he said. "Your father will take good care of you."

Wei flung the tears from his eyes. "Ba? He doesn't care about me! He doesn't even want me to learn opera!"

"He is only looking out for your future."

A few weeks later, Grandfather sailed for home, and then Ba's troupe went touring to seven towns. Wei stayed behind with the wardrobe master. He went to school and studied hard, hoping that high marks would please his father.

After a while, Wei asked when the singers would return.

"Whenever they earn enough to pay the bills," the wardrobe master sighed. "The crowds in this city are shrinking, so the troupe must travel up and down the coast looking for new audiences."

Wei wished that he were on the road with them, watching the company's shows, watching his father.

But when the company finally sputtered home in their run-down jalopies and rusty trucks, Wei was shocked. Ba's face and frame had lost weight, and coughing fits racked his body. The troupe was smaller, too, for two members had chosen to leave the company and return to China.

That night at dinner, Wei sat beside Ba and looked at the empty chairs, the meatless dish of vegetables and the broken kernels of rice. He heard how the tour had suffered from rain and feeble audiences, sore throats among the singers and the theft of a trunk of costumes. One truck had broken down on a lonely road and had to be towed into town.

But now the company planned to recover its losses by presenting a grand new opera. Ba attended rehearsals every night, refitted costumes and helped paint a new backdrop. All day long, he walked around memorizing new lyrics.

Wei pleaded to go with him to the theater as he had always done, but one glance at his father's dark face silenced him.

After school one afternoon, the rich boys of Chinatown called out, "What songs do beggars croak? You'll be singing them soon. Your company is almost bankrupt."

"Not so," retorted Wei. "We are doing a new show and painting backdrops. Crowds will come from across the country to watch."

"Fresh paint won't help when you're short of singers."

"We have plenty of voices," Wei told them, trying to sound confident.

"Hah! The best ones left for China and aren't coming back. People say your new show is stuck in the mud!"

Wei trudged home. If the company failed, Ba would lose work and lose face. And how could Wei ever become a star if there was no more opera company?

One evening close to opening night, Wei sneaked into the theater and hid behind the rows of seats. On the stage, musicians lined one side while singers filled the center with smooth, elegant movements. Wei saw two jeweled maidens hiding coyly behind delicate fans, a scholar and a porter carrying books and umbrellas, a boatman with long white whiskers and a priest wearing a golden crown.

But he didn't see Ba anywhere.

Wei crept under the seats to move closer and squinted at the faces.

He gasped. Ba wore a woman's
robe and waved its long sleeves. His
face had been painted pink; his eyes were
lined with black. But his voice kept cracking
as he tried singing the higher notes. The other
actors muttered impatiently, and the troupe master
stopped the music again and again.
Wei hurried home and pretended to be asleep when Ba
returned. He heard his father sigh and curse. He heard him hum
the new melody and then lose it in a fit of coughing.
That night, neither father nor son slept.

Early next morning, just when the black sky loosened into gray, Wei began to sing in a clear, strong voice. It was a woman's song, full of high, ringing notes.

Ba jumped from his bed and grabbed him. "Where did you learn that?"

"Grandfather taught me," Wei answered. "Shall we sing together?"

Wei let his jaw drop and waggled it loosely. Several times he curled his top lip like a pig's snout. He opened his mouth and let his tongue dart up and down, sideways and around in circles.

Grinning, Ba imitated him. Then they opened their mouths to sing.

After a few lines, Wei stopped and said, "Grandfather says the higher voice comes from the head, not the throat or chest. He always told me to roll the notes through my forehead."

Louder and louder the two pushed their voices. Over and over they practiced the woman's melody, until Ba sang it perfectly.

When they stopped for a rest, Ba told Wei the government had stopped Chinese immigration. Audiences were shrinking and actors now had to sing more than one role.

On opening night, Wei could hardly sit still. The crowd streamed in, jostling for good seats. An eager buzz filled the air, for a new show always excited the audiences. They brought in bags of dried plums and crunched on peanuts and sunflower seeds. A brass horn sounded and bright lamps lit the stage. Wei rubbed his cold hands to warm them.

A hush fell over the hall.

Two women glided onto the stage, rocking on tiny shoes. The audience murmured with approval at their dainty movements. Wei didn't recognize his father under the jeweled headdress, under the layers of make-up, under the flowing silks of pink and scarlet. But when Ba started to sing, Wei heard his grandfather's voice and his own soaring through the hall like a bell.

He didn't know whether there would
still be a Chinese opera when he grew up,
but on that night, he, too, was a star.